♡ Eva's Campfire Adventure ♡

Read more
OWL DIARIES
books!

OWL DIARIES

♡ Eva's Campfire Adventure ♡

Rebecca
Elliott

BRANCHES

SCHOLASTIC INC.

For our fabulous camping buddies
the Cheeseman family. xxx —R.E.

Copyright © 2020 by Rebecca Elliott

All rights reserved. Published by Scholastic Inc., *Publishers since 1920.* SCHOLASTIC, BRANCHES, and associated logos are trademarks and/or registered trademarks of Scholastic Inc.

The publisher does not have any control over and does not assume any responsibility for author or third-party websites or their content.

No part of this publication may be reproduced, stored in a retrieval system, or transmitted in any form or by any means, electronic, mechanical, photocopying, recording, or otherwise, without written permission of the publisher. For information regarding permission, write to Scholastic Inc., Attention: Permissions Department, 557 Broadway, New York, NY 10012.

This book is a work of fiction. Names, characters, places, and incidents are either the product of the author's imagination or are used fictitiously, and any resemblance to actual persons, living or dead, business establishments, events, or locales is entirely coincidental.

Library of Congress Cataloging-in-Publication Data

Names: Elliott, Rebecca, author. | Elliott, Rebecca. Owl Diaries.
Title: Eva's Campfire Adventure / Rebecca Elliott.
Description: First edition. | New York : Scholastic, Inc., 2020. | Series: Owl diaries | Summary: Eva Wingdale and her owl classmates are on a camping trip to the other side of the forest, where one of the assignments is to make useful inventions—but Eva and Lucy become totally distracted by the legend of Nellie Wingdale, founder of Treetopolis and her buried treasure, and never finish their project.
Identifiers: LCCN 2019020999 | ISBN 9781338298697 (paperback) | ISBN 9781338298710 (reinforced library binding)
Subjects: LCSH: Owls—Juvenile fiction. | Camping—Juvenile fiction. | Treasure troves—Juvenile fiction. | Diaries—Juvenile fiction. | CYAC: Owls—Fiction. | Camping—Fiction. | Buried treasure—Fiction. | Diaries—Fiction.

Classification: LCC PZ7.E45812 Eug 2020 | DDC [Fic]--dc23

LC record available at https://lccn.loc.gov/2019020999

Classification: LCC PZ7.E45812 Tr 2019 | DDC [Fic]—dc23 LC record available at https://lccn.loc.gov/2018053289

10 9 8 7 6 5 4 3 2 1   20 21 22 23 24

Printed in China   62
First edition, January 2020

Edited by Katie Carella
Book design by Maria Mercado

♡ Table of Contents ♡

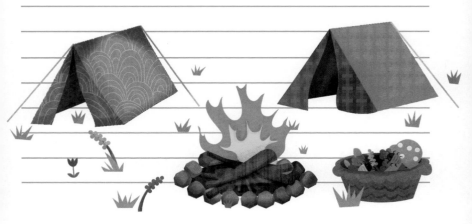

Woodpine Avenue

1

♡ Let's Go Camping! ♡

Sunday

Hi Diary,

Guess **HOO**! It's your favorite owl – Eva Wingdale!

This week I'm going CAMPING!

<u>I love</u>:

The sound of
rain on a tent

Candy

Nature watching

The word <u>backpack</u>

Packing for a trip

 Solving problems

Playing outside

 Sitting around
a campfire

I DO NOT love:

Rain leaking
through a tent

Candy sticking
to my feathers

Being stuck
indoors

The word <u>mud</u>

 Forgetting to pack something important

Impossible problems

 When friends snore

Mom's slug butter and jam sandwiches

This is my **OWLMAZING** family.

Dad

Mom

Humphrey

Baby Mo

Me

This is my pet bat, Baxter. He's such a cutie-pie.

I love being an owl!

We fly
almost silently.

We sleep in
the daytime.

Most owls **HOOT**, but some screech and some whinny like a horse!

HOOT!

SCREECH!

WHINNY

We love snuggling up together.

I live at number 11 Woodpine Avenue in Treetopolis.

My bestie, Lucy Beakman, lives next door.

11

9

My friends and I go to Treetop
Owlementary. Here is our class photo:

Jacob   Kiera   Lucy   Sue
Macy   Zara
Zac

Lilly   Hailey
        Me   Carlos
  George   Mrs. Featherbottom

My class is going on a camping trip!
I'm all packed.

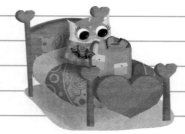

Now I must go to
sleep – so tomorrow
comes quicker!

♡ Campfire Fun ♡

Monday

Mrs. Featherbottom led the way to the campsite.

We weren't used to carrying such heavy backpacks, so we kept flying too close to the ground.

But we helped one another and got there in the end!

When we arrived, we got right to work.

George, Zara, Kiera, and Lilly set up the tents.

We will feel so cozy sleeping in these!

Carlos, Macy, and Sue gathered food for our dinner.

Hailey and Zac collected water from the river.

Lucy, Jacob, and I gathered logs to build a fire.

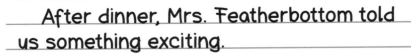

After dinner, Mrs. Featherbottom told us something exciting.

This week you have a project to complete. You'll work in pairs to build something <u>useful</u> out of materials you find in the forest.

Fun!

Will there be a prize for the best invention?

Yes! There will be a special trophy for the winners.

Ooooh!

We picked our partners.

I want that trophy! George, you're good at making things. You can be my partner.

Oh, okay.

Lucy and I chose to work together. We had NO idea what to make, but we knew we'd come up with something **OWLMAZING**!

Then we sat around the campfire toasting s'mores. YUM!

We **HOOTED** campfire songs.

We even sang a <u>special</u> version of my favorite song!

There was an owl who had a bat, and BAXTER was his name-o.
B–A–X–T–E-R
B–A–X–T–E-R
B–A–X–T–E-R
And Baxter was his name-o!

As the sun came up, we climbed into our sleeping bags. Our tents are so cozy! I don't think it will be long before we fall aslee . . . Zzzzzz.

♥ An OWLMAZING Discovery ♥

Tuesday

Tonight we woke up super-excited to start our forest projects.

Carlos and Zara searched for special feathers to make quill pens.

Sue and George looked for logs to make a catapult.

Hailey and Zac gathered pine needles to weave baskets.

Lilly and Jacob collected willow to make a hammock.

Macy and Kiera searched for sticks to hollow out to make flutes.

Everyone had great ideas. But Lucy and I had <u>NO</u> IDEAS!

Mrs. Featherbottom said we should all take a break and swim in the lake. It was such **FEATHER-SPLASHING** fun!

Then she told us a story: The Legend of Treetopolis. It was about Nellie Wingdale, the founder of Treetopolis.

Nellie Wingdale

Everyone went back to working on their projects.

But Lucy and I <u>still</u> didn't know what to make.

We need to get started!

You're right. Oh — something from the lake got stuck in your feathers.

Lucy pulled a reed from my feathers.

Then she had a **WING-CREDIBLE** idea!

We should make an umbrella out of reeds!

That's a great idea!

I had heard Hailey say there were lots of reeds by the river, so we went there to search. But when we got there, we found MUCH more than reeds!

Lucy! Do you see those old pebbles? It looks like they're in the shape of a letter!
Not a letter, Eva. An arrow!
There's another arrow!
FOLLOW THE ARROWS
OWL MY GOODNESS! IS THIS WHAT I THINK IT IS!?

Diary, we found one of Nellie Wingdale's TREASURE HUNT CLUES!!!

The arrows led deep into the forest.

We climbed into our sleeping bags.

Good day, Diary. Treasure hunters like us need all the sleep we can get!

♡ Follow the Clues! ♡

Wednesday

Tonight Mrs. Featherbottom surprised us with a cool activity: a forest obstacle course!

You and your project partner must work <u>together</u> to race through it.

30

She tied our wings together.

Ready, steady, go!

There were logs to crawl through,

stepping stones to jump across,

mud puddles to leap over,

and rope ladders to climb!

It was SO funny with our wings tied together! To be honest, I don't even know who won!

Afterward, while everyone else worked on their projects, Lucy and I went back to following arrows. We came out at a wide part of the river.

I don't see any more arrows. What do we do now?

Maybe this was all just someone's silly joke?

Wait, look at this!

Lucy found a clue carved into a rock:

The treasure you seek is on the other side.
But if you fly there, the clue will be denied.

So we have
to cross
the river.

But we're not
allowed to fly . . .

There was no way for us to cross the river without flying.

We told them about Nellie's clues. And we showed them the message in the rock.

The treasure you seek is on the other side. But if you fly there, the clue will be denied.

Then we all agreed to start the Treasure Hunters Club!

We began to row across the river.

Just then, our oar hit a tree stump!

We found a clue!

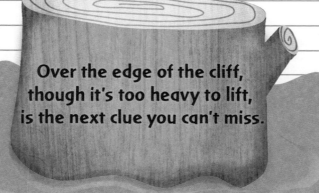

Over the edge of the cliff,
though it's too heavy to lift,
is the next clue you can't miss.

There's a cliff near here where
I was looking for feathers!
Follow me!

We looked over the cliff's edge and saw a boulder with a rope tied around it.

This <u>must</u> be the next clue!

Argh! What if we fall?!

You <u>can</u> fly you know!

Oh, yeah.

We flew down to the boulder.

I don't see a new message.

Maybe it's under the boulder.

Let's try lifting it. 1, 2, 3 — HEAVE!

We tried and tried. But it was WAY too heavy to lift.

The sun was nearly up, so we rushed back to camp.

We'll try again tomorrow.

Don't tell anyone else about our hunt though. I can't wait to surprise them with Nellie's treasure!

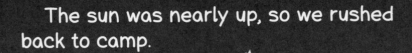

We all sat around the campfire.

Soon it was time to settle into our tents for the day. I felt bad for not telling Sue or any of the others about the treasure hunt.

I told Lucy how I was feeling.

Maybe we should tell them.

Let's just wait to see what we find tomorrow.

Yeah, we still might not even find anything!

Sue is right about our project though. We need to get to work!

When everyone else was asleep, we started weaving our umbrella. But we were too tired to get much work done.

Oh Diary, we'll never finish our project by Friday! But if we find the treasure, everyone will be <u>so</u> happy, it won't matter. Right? On the other **WING**, what if we <u>don't</u> find the treasure?!

5

♥ Let's All Pulley Together! ♥

Thursday

Tonight Mrs. Featherbottom took us on a nature walk. It was so much fun that I stopped worrying about the project and the treasure!

We learned how to identify footprints.

We made bark rubbings.

We went on
a bug hunt.

Zara drew a picture in the sand.

We found everything we needed. Then we got to work.

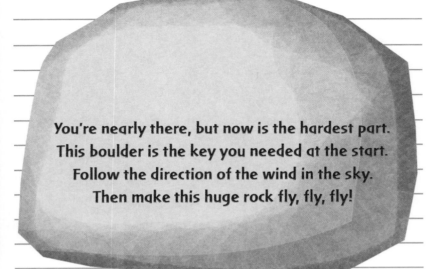

You're nearly there, but now is the hardest part.
This boulder is the key you needed at the start.
Follow the direction of the wind in the sky.
Then make this huge rock fly, fly, fly!

This rock is the <u>key</u>?
What does that mean?

How could we
make it f<u>ly</u>?

It's way too heavy
for us to throw it.

We brainstormed what to do next.

Lucy told us how to build a wind sock.

It's working!
The wind blows that way because of the mountains behind us.
Now what do we do?
I have no idea.

The sun was almost up. We still hadn't found the treasure AND none of us had finished our forest projects. How will we get everything done before we head home tomorrow?!

We whispered to one another around the campfire.

What should we do about our projects?

I know! We'll wake up before everyone else and work then.

Good plan.

So we'll finish our projects first thing tomorrow. Yay!

♡ Find That Treasure! ♡

Friday

DISASTER!

All six of us overslept! We had no time to finish our projects!

We watched everyone else show what they'd made . . .

The stick flutes sounded **HOOTIFUL**.

The hammock looked super comfy.

Even Sue and George's catapult was **OWLSOME**.

Then it was time for me and Lucy to share what we had made.

It was time for us Treasure Hunters to share our secret.

The thing is . . .

None of us have finished our projects.

Because we've been busy —

Searching for Nellie's hidden treasure!

Then Sue laughed. HA HA!

There isn't REALLY any treasure!

I couldn't believe Sue was laughing. Nellie's treasure IS real, and our club is going to prove it.

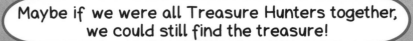
Maybe if we were all Treasure Hunters together, we could still find the treasure!

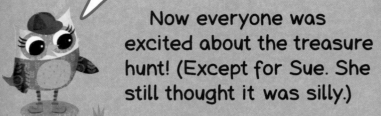
Now everyone was excited about the treasure hunt! (Except for Sue. She still thought it was silly.)

We read the last clue again.

You're nearly there, but now is the hardest part.
This boulder is the key you needed at the start.
Follow the direction of the wind in the sky.
Then make this huge rock fly, fly, fly!

The boulder flew across the river!

It landed on one
end of a strange log.
A smaller rock on the
other end rocketed
off the log.

The smaller rock
rolled down a hill. Finally,
it stopped at a hollowed-out tree
trunk. We crept inside and found . . .

NELLIE'S TREASURE!

The treasure you seek was already found.
It is the friends who helped you,
The family who support you,
The smarts you used to get here,
And the gifts of the forest all around.

I'm sorry I didn't believe in the treasure, Eva.

That's okay, Sue. It was pretty unbelievable!

So what should we do with the treasure?

We thought about our friends and families, the amazing things we have made, and the forest fun we've had on this trip. We knew what to do.

Let's leave the treasure here. And put the rocks back where we found them — so other campers can find Nellie's statue and message.

Agreed.

Mrs. Featherbottom told us she was proud of us and of the useful projects we had built. She said we were all winners! She gave us trophies filled with candy coins — our very own treasure!

It's a Treasure Hunters Party!